"I have great faith in a seed.

Convince me you have a seed there,

and I am prepared to expect wonders."

— HENRY DAVID THOREAU

Dear Young Readers,

This *Companion* to the book *Little Garlic—Enchanted Tales for all Ages* is for you to explore your own gifts. We are giving the example of a seed that grows into a beautiful tree that grows branches, leaves, flowers, and bears fruit. And, **you** are the chosen gardener of this tree.

As you explore this *Companion*, think of a tree that you particularly like and all the gifts that it provides: shade, nesting place for birds, contribution to the environment, beauty, flowers, and fruit.

Your growth can be like that tree. We are hoping that your experience working on this *Companion* will be the same. Just like Little Garlic, you will get in touch with your gifts a day at a time and nurture them as you go on your own journey.

A Note for Parents, Educators, and Adult Readers

This *Companion* to the book *Little Garlic— Enchanted Tales for all Ages* offers readers the chance to explore the lessons Little Garlic is learning on his journey in search of self: who he is and where he came from. It is also a flexible resource for those who wish to support readers of all ages. As such, the activities have been designed for everyone to be able to think and engage more deeply with the wisdom of *Little Garlic*.

We hope that *Little Garlic* and the *Companion* evoke a sense of wonder and awe in its readers and provide a medium to get in touch with one's own inner wisdom, gifts, beauty, love, and all that is held sacred and meaningful.

For each story in *Little Garlic*, we offer seven options for further engagement. We have suggested a *Theme*, a *Quote*, and a *Special Word* which we think are particularly reflective of the story. For each of those, we also invite readers to share the theme, quote, or special word that resonates most deeply for them.

These activities may be used as ways to reflect independently; as discussion starters; or to make connections among the stories. Participants in a book club may be invited to share a special passage that has been meaningful to them; educators might start a class discussion by asking each student to share the one word that most stood out for them from the stories that were just read. Parents may wish to have a family conversation around any of the components of the *Companion* and use the guided meditations as a nice end-of-the-day nurturing and soothing family activity.

Any, or all, of the activities for any of the stories may be used, and we invite you to consider what works best for you, your family, your readers, or students. There is space throughout this companion where readers can engage with our prompts. You might find it even more helpful to suggest a journal for further space to write or draw.

The *Questions for Reflection* section invites readers to engage in conversations with themselves and others about the life-lessons that Onion and Little Garlic are learning for themselves.

The *Experience* section includes questions which may be posed around a kitchen table, a morning circle, or in a community room. They may also serve as prompts for journaling for readers of all ages to apply the stories of Onion and Little Garlic to their own lives. The *Art* section includes prompts for drawing, so that readers can also process the lessons of Onion and Little Garlic with images. These prompts could also provide journaling opportunities related to the themes of each chapter.

The *Guided Meditations* section provides guided meditations which can be used with a small or large group of readers. If you are well practiced in leading guided meditations, feel free to use these as a guide. If you are new to leading guided meditations, it would be helpful to practice before you lead. Use a soft, calm voice, and take more time in reading through the meditation. It would be helpful to pause at times to provide your meditators with time to engage with the meditation.

At the end of the *Companion*, we have included two additional pages, "My Special Tree" and "My Gratitude Journal." These are opportunities to reflect on what nurtures us in life.

Little Garlic is on a journey. He begins by gazing outward; but with the support of Magic Wind and his good friend and guide Onion, Little Garlic begins to understand that he will not find outside of himself the answers to the questions he is asking. This *Companion* invites readers to focus their gaze inward, connecting to themselves and our shared humanity.

Table of Contents

How to use your *Companion*   4

   Activities included in this book!

The following chapters correspond to the chapters in
Little Garlic: Enchanted Tales for All Ages

Chapter 1	**The Special Meeting**	6
Chapter 2	**The Ancestors**	11
Chapter 3	**Magic Wind**	16
Chapter 4	**The Story of Lotus Blossum**	21
Chapter 5	**The Story of Rambutan**	26
Chapter 6	**The Story of Caterpillar**	32
Chapter 7	**The Story of Morning Glory**	37
Chapter 8	**The Story of Strawberry**	42
Chapter 9	**Little Garlic's Special Dream**	47
Chapter 10	**The Story of Adam**	52
Chapter 11	**The Flower of Peace**	57

My Special Tree   62

My Gratitude Journal   64

The Flower of Peace Poem   65

Words and images excerpted or inspired by *Little Garlic: Enchanted Tales for All Ages*.
Wyatt-MacKenzie Publishing

How to use your Companion

A Theme

We have suggested a **theme** for each story, and we have left a space for you to think, write, and draw what you think the theme is.

A Quote

We have also included a sample **quote** from each story. Perhaps, you would like to choose a quote from each story that speaks to you and write it in the space that has been provided.

Questions for Reflection

We have written **questions** for you to think about. These questions provide further understanding about each story. We invite you to use your imagination in thinking about the questions. Allow your mind to be open to wonder.

Special Word

We have selected a "**special word**" from each story and encourage you to see if there is a word in each story that is especially meaningful to you. After you have chosen your "special word" in each story, think about what it means to you and what it will mean on your own journey of personal growth.

Art

Visualize that word as if it were an **ornament**: its shape, color, form, etc. and draw it on the ornament page. Your ornament is a symbol of what that word means to you. Engage your imagination. How you visualize and draw your word is up to you, and it can be whatever you choose it to be: a flower, bird, person, landscape, or anything! These ornaments will be your companions that you will nurture and look after as you walk along your own journey.

Add to your Companion

Your Special Tree
Each life is like a seed and when nurtured it can grow into a special tree. For this to happen, it is important to be grateful for all that nurtures us.

To help you think about your own life, and how it can grow in this way, we have included a "Tree of Ornaments" page at the end for you to visualize and draw your special tree and what nurtures it. The ornaments you have drawn are examples of what can nurture your life.

Continue Your Growth ~ Start a Gratitude Journal
And finally, as Little Garlic learned, being grateful for all that nurtures us is important in helping us to grow. So, we have suggested that in addition to using your *Companion*, you start a Gratitude Journal as a way for you to be in touch with all that nurtures you each day.

**The world awaits *you* and
your world of gifts and wonderment!**

Let's get started ...

Theme of **The Special Meeting**

Onion invites Little Garlic to tell his story of where he came from and why he is all alone and sad. Onion shares his own story as well. Good friends who listen are important in our lives in developing our own special gifts.

Is there another theme that you see? Share it here:

Quote

"Don't worry little fella, I'm here for you. Why don't you start from the very beginning and tell me your story."

Is there another quote that you like? If so, write it down here:

Special Word

Here is one suggested special word that is important: **Friendship**.

Is there another word that you think is important, a word that was especially meaningful for you as you read or heard the story? Write it down here:

Questions for Reflection

What do you do when you feel alone or sad? Do you talk to anyone (like a family member, friend, teacher, or even your pet)?

What qualities do you most value in a friend?

Did you learn an important lesson in this story?

Have you been a good friend to anyone who needed to share their story?

Experience

How would you tell your own story? You can share your reflections with another person or write about it here or in your journal.

Art

Next, can you turn this into artwork? Visualize what **friendship** means to you. What is a good friend like? What does friendship look like? What does it feel like to be in a friendship, or to be a friend? Draw it as you like in the circle above. This is a symbol of what friendship means to you. Friendship will be an ornament for you to keep, nurture, and share on your journey.

Guided Meditation

Relax in a comfortable position and gently close your eyes. Relax your head, your face, your neck, your back, your arms, your hands, your fingers, your legs, and your toes. Release any tension you may have.

Become aware of your breathing. Feel your breath and follow your breath as you gently inhale and exhale. Feel the rise and fall of your chest and abdomen as you slowly inhale and slowly exhale.

With each slow breath take in all that is good. Feel all that goodness move throughout your body, from your head all the way to your toes.

As you exhale, breathe out all the things that bothered you during the day. Breathe it all out.

Repeat as many times as you like.

Visualize yourself in a beautiful field of flowers. The sky is blue, and the sun's warmth is comforting. You can hear the chirping of the birds in the distance. You can smell the the scent of the flowers as the gentle breeze settles on your face.

Now, relax completely and recall one thing that you are grateful for today. Let that feeling of gratitude fill your heart and let that wonderful feeling expand and fill you from your head to your toes. Keep that feeling of gratitude with you throughout the day and night.

Pause

Now, gently open your eyes and become aware of your body and surroundings. Take a few minutes before you gently and slowly get back up.

With that feeling of gratitude in your heart, feel how wonderful it is to be given the gift of life.

"Now that I have gotten to know myself,
I understand others much better."

The Ancestors

Theme of The Ancestors

Onion tells Little Garlic about the value of his ancestors. The strengths, special gifts, legacies of your ancestors can give you a strong foundation in discovering how special you are.

What is another theme that you see? Share it here:

Quote

"Your appearance tells me that your origins—that is your very, very beginnings—are in the mountains in a very distant place. As to why you're here, I know for sure that you were brought here for a special purpose."

Is there another quote that you like? If so, write it down here:

Special Word

Here is one suggested special word that is important: **Faith**: faith in how special you are and how you will be able to develop your special gifts.

Is there another word that you think is important? A word that was particularly meaningful for you as you read or heard the story? Write it down here:

Questions for Reflection

Can you think of any values and strengths that have come to you from your ancestors?

Can you think as far back as you can and think of how they contributed to the good of the world?

The Ancestors

Experience

Think of all the values and contributions that your ancestors have made.
It can be anything: something very small or great. It can be their values, hard work, raising families, creativity, contribution to their communities, making a difference in the lives of others, etc.

Bring them to your mind and think about how their values, strength, and love have made a difference in your life. Then, tell that as a story. You can share your reflections with another person or write about it here, or in your journal.

Art

Next, can you turn this into artwork? Visualize what **faith** means to you. What does it look like to have faith in how special you are? What does it look like to have faith in how you will be able to develop your special gifts?

Draw it above and color it. Remember, this is a symbol of what faith means to you. Faith will be another ornament for you to keep, nurture, and share on your journey.

Guided Meditation

Relax in a comfortable position and gently close your eyes. Relax your head, your face, your neck, your back, your arms, your hands, your fingers, your legs, and your toes. Release any tension or tiredness you may have.

Become aware of your breathing. Feel your breath and follow your breath as you gently inhale and exhale. Feel the rise and fall of your chest and abdomen as you slowly inhale and slowly exhale.

With each slow breath take in all that is good. Feel all that goodness move throughout your body, from your head all the way to your toes.

As you exhale, breathe out all the things that bothered you during the day. Breathe it all out.

Now relax. Relax completely.

Now, visualize you are a seed that sends roots deep into the ground. These roots are necessary to provide a strong foundation for you. The seed must toil hard and overcome all the obstacles that are on its way. It must have patience and endurance to grow roots and push out from under the ground so that it can be nurtured by the sun and grow branches, leaves, flowers, and fruit.

The fruit is the result of the seed's hope, toil, and endurance.

As you journey through the day, you are building your strong foundation for the next day by your good work, good thoughts, and good words. These are like seeds that will grow and nurture you as you journey through life.

Pause

Now, bring your attention back to your breath and slowly inhale and gently exhale. Repeat this several times. See how wonderful it is to feel peaceful and hopeful. Your journey is just beginning, just like a seed, just like the journey of Little Garlic.

Pause

Now, gently open your eyes and become aware of your body and surroundings. Take a few minutes before you gently and slowly get back up.

Find confidence in your worth and value.

Theme of Magic Wind

Good, as well as difficult, experiences teach us important lessons in life.

What is another theme that you see? Share it here:

Quote

"Magic Wind knows where to take us, but we really have to want to be on the journey and have a little trust in Magic Wind."

Is there another quote that you like? If so, write it down here:

Special Word

Here is one suggested special word that is important in this story: **Trust**: that we can learn from both good and difficult experiences.

Is there another word that you think is important? A word that was meaningful for you as you read or heard the story? Write it down here:

Questions for Reflection

Can you think of an experience that was difficult but from which you learned an important lesson?

Can you think of a good experience you had from which you learned an important lesson?

Have there been points on your journey when you have felt like you have been guided by Magic Wind? What was that experience like?

Experience

Bring to your mind the journey you have been on so far. As you witness that journey, do you feel sometimes you were guided by Magic Wind to be where you were? Was there anyone who helped you to listen to that guidance? You can share your reflections with another person or write about it here or in your journal.

Art

Next, can you turn this into artwork? Visualize how **trust** in whatever happens to you will teach you important lessons on your journey and growth. Draw it as you like in the circle above and color it. This is a symbol of what trust means to you. Trust will be another ornament for you to keep, nurture, and share on your journey.

Guided Meditation

Close your eyes, slowly inhale and gently exhale. Find a comfortable place for your hands: on your stomach, at your sides, resting on your heart.

Notice the physical sensations of your breath. Perhaps you feel the breath as it enters your body through your nostrils, the rise and fall of your chest, the expansion and contraction of your stomach. Just notice the rhythm of your breath.

Become aware of the contact your body is making (with the bed, floor, chair). Embrace the feeling of support. Allow your muscles to soften and release any tension you may have from the day.

Let's begin by extending goodness to yourself.

Repeat these phrases in your mind: *May I be healthy. May I be kind. May I be at peace.*

May I be healthy. May I be kind. May I be at peace.

Now bring to mind someone you love. Perhaps a parent, friend, teacher, or pet.

*May **you** be healthy.*

*May **you** be kind.*

*May **you** be at peace.*

And then radiate goodness from your heart all over the world, spreading upward to the skies, and downwards to the deepest depths of the ocean.

May all beings be healthy. May all beings be kind. May all beings be at peace.

Pause

Now, gently begin to feel your breath as you slowly inhale and exhale. Bring your attention back to your body and see how wonderful you feel.

When you are ready, wiggle your fingers and toes, give yourself a good stretch, and open your eyes.

When we celebrate our individual uniqueness, we feel whole and complete, and we don't feel lonely or insecure anymore.

The Story of Lotus Blossom

Theme of The Story of Lotus Blossom

By nurturing hope and love, we can develop endurance and strength under the most difficult situations.

What is another theme that you see? Share it here:

Quote

"We nurture love and hope in our heart every day to endure life in the swamp. Otherwise, we wouldn't have the strength to overcome the difficulties."

Is there another quote that you like? If so, write it down here:

Special Word

Here is one suggested special word: **Endurance**

Is there another word that you think is important, a word that was meaningful for you as you read or heard the story? Write it down here:

The Story of Lotus Blossom

Questions for Reflection

Has something you thought was bad ever turned into something good? Did that surprise you?

What do you think Lotus Blossom meant by "purity of heart" and "clarity of mind"? Why would she tell Little Garlic that these qualities are important to develop?

How might these qualities help someone going on a journey to discover who they are?

The Story of Lotus Blossom

Experience

Write about experiences that have made you who you are. This is an opportunity to reflect on your past experiences and capture your special memories.

Begin by writing down examples of the following:

Two important experiences that have influenced you: one difficult and one happy

Two people who have helped you through difficult experiences

Two or more words that best describe who you are

Two or more words that best describe your hopes

Two or more things you value the most

Two or more words that describe what makes you special

The Story of Lotus Blossom

Art

Next, can you turn this into artwork? Visualize how **endurance** can be an everlasting friend and how it can help you develop the strength you need to cultivate your gifts even when it is very difficult. Draw it and color it as you see it in the circle above. This is a symbol of what endurance means to you. Endurance will be another ornament for you to keep, nurture, and share on your journey.

The Story of Lotus Blossom

Guided Meditation

Lotus Blossom reminds us that no matter where we find ourselves, in a swamp or a backyard pond, we can be beautiful.

Relax in a comfortable position and gently close your eyes. Relax your head, your face, your neck, your back, your arms, your hands, your fingers, your legs, and your toes. Release any tension that you may be holding.

Become aware of your breathing. Feel your breath and follow your breath as you gently inhale and exhale. Feel the rise and fall of your chest and abdomen as you slowly inhale and slowly exhale, just like a wave slowly rising and falling.

With each slow breath take in all that is good. Feel all that goodness move throughout your body, from your head all the way to your toes.

As you exhale, breathe out all the things that bothered you during the day. Breathe it all out.

Repeat as many times as you like.

Now, visualize how Lotus Blossom would see you. Do you see how it feels to see yourself as Lotus Blossom sees you? Does she see you with loving eyes?

Visualize that you are looking at yourself in a mirror with the eyes of Lotus Blossom. How does that feel? Stay with this feeling and let it be yours.

Pause

Now, gently open your eyes and become aware of your body and surroundings. Write down any words or thoughts that came to mind as you saw yourself through the eyes of Lotus Blossom, as you saw what makes you, you.

Create an affirmation (a supportive statement) based on the words that came to your mind as you saw yourself through the eyes of Lotus Blossom. The next time you are overwhelmed repeat that phrase in your mind to remind yourself of how special you are.

For example, when Little Garlic tells Lotus Blossom that she is beautiful, she could turn that into an affirmation, "I am beautiful."

With a feeling of gratitude, see how wonderful it is to be YOU! There is no one else like you: you are unique.

I am special.

The Story of Rambutan

Theme of **The Story of Rambutan**

Do not look at the outward appearance but look at the inward beauty in yourself and others.

What is another theme that you see? Share it here:

Quote

"Rambutan: 'We know that we look ugly and scary at first, but our beauty is inside and has to be discovered.'"

Is there another quote that you like? If so, write it down here:

Special Word

Here is one suggested special word: **Beauty**

Is there another word that you think is important, a word that was meaningful to you as you read or heard the story? Write it down here:

Questions for Reflection

Have you ever been frightened of something based on what you think it might be like, before you knew what it really was?

How did you feel when you found out that you may have judged something or someone incorrectly? What did you do?

Sometimes we need someone else, a parent, friend, teacher, or classmate to point out how beautiful we really are. Who has helped you realize your beauty?

Experience

If you were to look at yourself the way the teacher showed Rambutan how to see his beauty, how would you see yourself? Now look at yourself with new eyes and see your beauty. You can share your reflections with another person or write about it here or in your journal.

The Story of Rambutan

Art

Next, can you turn this into artwork? Visualize how **beauty** can be seen in someone if they don't seem to be beautiful at first. Draw it and color it as you like in the circle above. This is a symbol of what beauty means to you. Beauty will be another ornament for you to keep, nurture and share on your journey.

Guided Meditation

Make yourself comfortable and gently close your eyes. Relax your head, your face, your neck, your back, your arms, your hands, your fingers, your legs, and your toes. Release any tension you may be holding.

Become aware of your breathing. Feel your breath and follow your breath as you gently inhale and exhale. Feel the rise and fall of your chest and abdomen as you slowly inhale and slowly exhale.

Pause

Imagine yourself in a place that is beautiful and peaceful, your special place. Picture it clearly. What does it look like? What do you see? Do you hear any sounds? Are there any scents or fragrances? What time of year is it? What makes this place special? Feel yourself in that place. Do you feel happy there?

What does happy feel like? How do you know when you are happy? We will explore where in our body feelings live.

Gently take a deep breath and gently release. Become aware of the physical sensations of your breath.

Perhaps you notice the air as it enters your body through your nostrils, the rise and fall of your chest, the expansion and contraction of your stomach. Just notice the rhythm of your breath.

Pause

Recall a time when you were truly happy, make the image as vivid as you can, picture where you were and what you were doing.

Notice what happens in your body: did a smile settle across your face, do you feel warm, or cool, is there a particular place that happiness lives in your body, is it a lightness at the top of your head, a warmth that radiates from your heart; just notice.

Pause

Bring your attention back to your breath, notice the physical sensations of breathing, the air as it enters your body through your nostrils, the rise and fall of your chest, the expansion and contraction of your stomach.

Whenever you need to, you can connect with this feeling. Just close your eyes and bring your attention to your breath. Happiness is always there waiting for you.

When you are ready, wiggle your fingers and toes, give yourself a good stretch, and open your eyes.

See others for who they are.

The Story of Caterpillar

Theme of The Story of Caterpillar

Don't be discouraged by long periods during which you don't see progress in developing your special gifts; nurture hope and patience.

What is another theme that you see? Share it here:

Quote

"When I had lost all hope, suddenly you showed up!
I didn't think anyone would offer to help me. But now I feel so lucky!
You're going to help me. I don't feel scared and alone anymore."

Is there is another quote that you like? If so, write it down here:

Special Word

Here is one suggested special word: **Hope**

Is there another word that you think is important, a word that was meaningful for you as you read or heard the story? Write it down here:

Questions for Reflection

What is now will not be in the future. How have you changed since you were little?

Does growth mean change for you? Does change mean growth for you? Do you welcome change or do you fear it? Why?

When Caterpillar finds itself in trouble, along comes Onion. Has anyone helped you become who you are today? How?

What does hope mean to you? Has hope been a friend to you during difficult times?

Experience

A great transformation allowed Caterpillar to become a Butterfly. Write a letter to your younger self. What would you want your younger self to know that you have learned?

Dear Younger Me,

You can share your reflections with another person or write about it here or in your journal.

The Story of Caterpillar

Art

Next, can you turn this into artwork? Visualize **hope**; what does hope look like? What does hope mean to you? How has hope been a friend to you? What helps you to have hope? Draw what hope looks like to you and color it. Hope will be another ornament for you to keep, nurture, and share on your journey.

Guided Meditation

Close your eyes, slowly take a deep breath, and slowly release. Find a comfortable place for your hands: on your stomach, at your sides, resting on your heart. Notice the rhythm of your breath.

Become aware of the contact your body is making (with the bed, floor, chair). Embrace the feeling of support. Allow your muscles to soften and release any tension you may be holding onto from the day.

Now visualize hope as a seed in your heart. Water the seed of hope with a good thought each morning when you wake up. Watch that seed slowly open in your heart. As you go through the day, with each positive thought, word, or deed, the flower of hope opens its blossom and embraces your heart.

Hope is your flower. You can see it in any shape, form, or color. Draw it in your mind's eye and see it as your radiant and beautiful flower that will always be with you.

Whenever you feel alone or sad, or you need help to get through the day, reach within your heart and see your flower of hope. Let your flower of hope be your friend through the day.

Pause

When you are ready, take a slow deep breath and slowly exhale. Now, gently open your eyes, become aware of your body and surroundings, and give yourself a good stretch. Take a few minutes before you gently and slowly get back up.

Remember hope is always in your heart!

**Celebrate change, hope,
transformation, trust, and belief.**

Little Garlic
The Story of Morning Glory

Theme of The Story of Morning Glory

Deep love and prayer for others is an important part of our growth in life.

What is another theme that you see? Share it here:

Quote

"The little boy loved Morning Glory so much that he poured all his love into prayers to bring her back to life."

Is there another quote that you like? If so, write it down here:

Special Word

Here is one suggested special word: **Prayer**

Is there is another word that you think is important, a word that was meaningful to you as you read or heard the story? Write it down here:

Questions for Reflection

Little Garlic is going to share his dream with Onion. Do you remember your dreams?

What do you do when a friend is not feeling well?

What do you do when you need support/strength?

The boy prayed for Morning Glory. What does prayer mean to you?

Does prayer help you open your heart with love for others?

The Story of Morning Glory

Experience

Morning Glory knows that she was able to get well because of her friend's love and prayers. How might you pray from deep within your heart for others or for the world in a way that shows your love for them? How might you pray from deep within your heart for yourself? You can write your prayer here, or say it, out loud or in your heart.

The Story of Morning Glory

Art

Next, can you turn this into artwork? Visualize **prayer**. What can prayer mean to you? What can prayer mean to someone you care about? What can prayer mean to someone in need? Draw it and color it as you like in the circle above. This is a symbol of what prayer means to you. Prayer will be another ornament for you to keep, nurture, and share on your journey.

The Story of Morning Glory

Guided Meditation

Close your eyes, and gently take a deep breath in and slowly release. Find a comfortable place for your hands: on your stomach, at your side, resting on your heart. Notice the physical sensations of your breath.

Perhaps you feel the breath as it enters your body through your nostrils, the rise and fall of your chest, the expansion and contraction of your stomach. Just notice the rhythm of your breath.

Become aware of the contact your body is making (with the bed, floor, chair). Embrace the feeling of support. Allow your muscles to soften and release any tension you may be holding onto from the day.

Bring your attention to your heart. Place your hands one over the other on your heart and feel the pulse in your heart. Notice the connection of your heart and your breath.

Repeat the word love as you breathe in, focusing your attention on your heart. On the out breath imagine love strengthened by your heart extending outward.

Now, send prayer from your heart outward as you exhale.

Prayer is radiating out from your heart.

Imagine someone who needs help: it could be a friend, family member, a pet, or even yourself. Connect to that person in your heart.

Feel love for that person in your heart.

Prayer is radiating from your heart and expanding.

Continue to breathe and feel love expanding in your heart and prayer radiating out. Rest in this wonderful feeling and the goodness it brings to you and to others.

Pause

When you are ready, take a slow deep breath and exhale. Gently open your eyes, become aware of your body and surroundings, and give yourself a good stretch. Take a few minutes before you gently and slowly get back up.

Love nurtures all things.

The Story of Strawberry

Theme of **The Story of Strawberry**

Nurturing love in the heart opens a world of wonder, joy, and beauty.

What is another theme that you see? Share it here:

Quote

"The source of love in the heart is always there because it's connected to everlasting love …. When we are mindful of this love, we treat others with kindness, compassion, respect, understanding, and all the goodness that's in our heart …. It also helps us not to judge others but to see the value in all things."

Is there another quote that you like? If so, write it down here:

Special Word

Here is one suggested special word: **Love**

Is there another word that you think is important, a word that was meaningful for you as you read or heard the story? Write it down here:

Questions for Reflection

Strawberry talks about "real love." What do you think she means?

Why do you think people fight with each other?

How does love influence how we treat others?

Experience

Strawberry tells Onion that the love in his heart is connected to everlasting love. Visualize your heart's connection to everlasting love. How might the love in your heart help you to practice friendship, learn to trust, and endure challenges? How might the love in your heart help you to have hope, or see beauty? You can share your reflections with another person or write about it here or in your journal.

The Story of Strawberry

Art

Next, can you turn this into artwork? See what **love** means to you, and what it could mean to someone else. Draw it and color it as you like in the circle above. This is a symbol of what love means to you. Love will be another ornament for you to keep, nurture, and share on your journey.

The Story of Strawberry

Guided Meditation

Close your eyes, slowly take a deep breath, and slowly release. Find a comfortable place for your hands, on your stomach, at your sides, resting on your heart. Notice the rhythm of your breath.

Become aware of the contact your body is making (with the bed, floor, chair). Embrace the feeling of support. Allow your muscles to soften and release any tension you may be holding onto from the day.

Relax completely and imagine yourself in a place that is loving. Picture clearly where you are; it can be anywhere. What does that place look like? What do you hear around you? What makes this place so special? Feel yourself in that place.

Take a moment now to feel what love means to you. Picture vividly your own love and how you share it.

What does love feel like in your heart?

Everlasting love is always present, has no boundary or limit. Can you visualize what everlasting love feels like?

Now visualize your love connected with everlasting love. What does that connection feel like? Feel that connection in your heart.

Focus on that connection and feel everlasting love embracing you and supporting you. Your heart is connected to everlasting love.

Feel this connection. You can nurture and strengthen this connection with everlasting love every day by coming back to this connection.

When you are ready, take a slow deep breath and exhale. Gently open your eyes, become aware of your body and surroundings, and give yourself a good stretch. Take a few minutes before you gently and slowly get back up.

Love is with me and in my heart.

Little Garlic's Special Dream

Theme of Little Garlic's Special Dream

There is a "Secret Star" within every heart that with the help of Magic Wind, can guide us.

What is another theme that you see? Share it here:

Quote

"Everyone has this brightest of stars in their own heart, and it's through this star that they can find their own secret treasure and experience true love."

Is there another quote that you like? If so, write it down here:

Special Word

Here is one suggested special word: **Secret Star**

Is there another word that you think is important? A word that was meaningful for you as you read or heard the story? Write it down here:

Questions for Reflection

Can you recall a special dream that you have had?

Have you ever learned something from a dream?

Experience

Do you ever wake up with a special feeling from your dream? Do you sometimes feel that something meaningful happened in your dream? What does that feel like? You can share your experience with another person or write about it here or in your journal.

Little Garlic's Special Dream

Art

You can turn this into artwork. Visualize **Secret Star** in your heart. Draw it and color it as you like. This is a symbol of what Secret Star means to you. Secret Star will be another ornament for you to keep, nurture, and share on your journey.

Little Garlic's Special Dream

Guided Meditation

Relax in a comfortable position and gently close your eyes. Relax your head, your face, your neck, your back, your arms, your hands, your fingers, your legs, and your toes. Relax any tension you may have.

Become aware of your breathing. Feel your breath and follow your breath as you gently inhale and exhale. Feel the rise and fall of your chest and abdomen as you slowly inhale and slowly exhale.

Visualize the night sky, filled with stars, so magical, so wondrous! Take a few moments to visualize the wonder that is the night sky. See what you notice. Allow your gaze to scan the sky and feel that wonder in your heart.

When you're completely relaxed, do you see what it feels like? Feel the light from the stars embrace you and protect you.

Feel the gentleness of the night breeze settle on your face and the wonder of the sky fill your heart. See how wonderful it is to be connected to all the stars.

Now, take a moment and open your heart to Secret Star. Feel the light of your Secret Star slowly radiate in your heart and expand.

As you inhale take this light into your heart, and as you exhale feel the light fill your body. Feel the warmth and peace of this light.

With each inhalation and exhalation feel the light radiate around you.

Feel the loving light of Secret Star embrace you.

The light of Secret Star is always present. You carry it with you. You can connect with it simply by placing your hands on your heart and taking a breath.

Gently inhale from your heart and as you exhale radiate your light out into the world, allow it to fill all the places that exist beyond you. Your light is infinite; sharing it creates more space for it to grow.

When you're ready, take a deep breath, remembering your connection to the expansive universe. Slowly open your eyes and see how wondrous you feel.

Know that you can always come back to this place of love and connection with Secret Star.

We are connected to the vast universe.

The Story of Adam

Theme of **The Story of Adam**

Our mission in life is to discover our secret gift—a seed that grows to completion. This is each person's unique treasure.

What is another theme that you see? Write it down here:

Quote

"'Adam,' she said, you're a brave young man. I've been waiting for you. You are a special young man with an important mission! I'm to give you a special gift, one that gives you the secret to peace."

Is there another quote that you like? If so, write it down here:

Special Word

Here are suggested special words: **special gift** or **special mission**.

Is there another word that you think is important, a word that was meaningful for you as you read or heard the story? Write it down here:

Questions for Reflection

Why do you think people can be mean to people they label different from themselves?

Have you ever been unkind to someone because you thought they were different?

What does it feel like to be cared for by someone?

Experience

On his journey, Adam experienced many friends who helped him. Who are the friends in your life who help you on your journey? Have you been a good friend to someone on their journey? You can share your reflections with another person or write about it here or in your journal.

Art

Next, can you turn this into artwork? Visualize your **special gift**. What is the special gift that is unique to you? Draw and color it as you like above. This is a symbol of what you would like to share with others or the world. Your special gift will be another ornament for you to keep, nurture, and share on your journey.

The Story of Adam

Guided Meditation

Find a comfortable place to sit or lie down and gently close your eyes. Take a deep breath in, and on the release, let go of any tension you may be holding in your body. Take another deep breath in and settle into this moment, setting your intention that you will be present. Let go of any thoughts, worries, or concerns.

Allow your breath to return to its normal rhythm. Notice the physical sensations of your breath, the air as it moves through your nostrils … the rise and fall of your chest, the expansion and contraction of your stomach. Become aware of the flow of your breath as you inhale and exhale.

Open your awareness to the world around you. Welcome any sensations that you notice, any sounds, smells, feelings that call to your attention. Just notice, don't try to shut out any of the sensations, welcome them and allow your attention to rest with whatever you are noticing for as long as it calls for your attention.

Meditation expands our understanding of ourselves and the world around us.

For the next few moments just breathe and expand your awareness. Accept what is, as it is.

Visualize your special gift. Remember your special gift is unique to you. Everyone has a special gift. See how you would like to share your special gift.

Pause

When you are ready, wiggle your fingers and toes, give yourself a good stretch, and open your eyes.

Love is like the sun that nurtures and strengthens.

The Flower of Peace

Theme of **The Flower of Peace**

There is a connection between endurance and peace. By enduring hardships through patience and hope, and by nurturing compassion, love, and kindness in our heart the flower of peace will grow in our heart.

What is another theme you see? Write it down here:

Quote

"unless I went on this journey, I would never discover all that I have inside of me. She said that when the seed is separated, it knows that it has to overcome many obstacles by itself to survive and become a fruit or a flower …. One day his travels would take him to a secret garden …. This is where you will enter the garden of paradise and be blessed with eternal love."

Is there another quote that you like? If so, write it down here:

Special Word

Here is one suggested special word: **Peace**

Is there another word that you think is important, a word that was meaningful for you as you read or heard the story? Write it down here:

Questions for Reflection

Is it hard to say goodbye? Why/why not?

At first the seed depends on others, the birds and the wind, to carry it away from home. When it first finds itself alone, it is dark and scary, but out of the darkness a flower emerges. Do you think Little Garlic is ready to let go and continue the journey without Onion as a guide?

The Flower of Peace

Experience

In what ways are you a seed, still growing and learning from your experiences? What do you do to nurture your heart to be at peace? In what ways are you beginning to flower or to bear fruit? Are there ways that you can be a support to others as they grow? You can share your reflections with another person or write about it here or in your journal.

The Flower of Peace

Art

Next, can you turn this into artwork. Visualize the **Flower of Peace** and what it means to you. Draw that flower and color it as you like above. Your Flower of Peace will be another ornament for you to keep, nurture, and share on your journey.

The Flower of Peace

Guided Meditation

Relax in a comfortable position and gently close your eyes. Relax your head, your face, your neck, your back, your arms, your hands, your fingers, your legs, and your toes. Release any tension you may have.

Become aware of your breathing. Feel your breath and follow your breath as you gently inhale and exhale. Feel the rise and fall of your chest and abdomen as you slowly inhale and slowly exhale.

Imagine yourself in a place of peace. Picture clearly where you are (it can be anywhere) it is your special place. What does that place look like? What does it smell like? What do you hear around you? What makes this place peaceful? Feel yourself in that place.

Now imagine yourself holding the Flower of Peace. See the Flower of Peace clearly. What does it look like? What does it feel like in your hand? How do you feel holding it?

As you gaze at the Flower of Peace, think of the ways you have become who you are today. What obstacles have you overcome? Who have you met along the way who gave you support? For what have you been grateful? What have you learned through your heart?

As you continue to gaze at the Flower of Peace, think about the ways in which you are still a seed. What do you need to keeping growing? Are there people in your life who can support you as you grow? Do you spend time listening to your heart to help you grow? Take some time to reflect about this.

Welcome the start of each day,
      with a feeling of love in your heart
      nurture this love as you go through the day
      with a kind deed for someone in need
      a smile and kind words for all those you meet.

Remember to nurture your heart with hope, faith, beauty, and love each day
      until the seed of peace blossoms in your heart and becomes the
      Flower of Peace that you offer to the world.

The world is waiting for you.

My Special Tree

Visualize yourself as a seed that can grow into a beautiful strong tree with deep roots in the earth, and a strong trunk and branches under the sky being nurtured by the sun.

On the opposite page—on your "Special Tree"—fill in the ornaments that you have drawn for each story with as many details as you like. Or, you can write the "special word" from each of the stories to hang on your tree.

Nurture each ornament as often as possible and watch how each one becomes stronger as you go on your journey. You can add to the drawing of your tree with words or images that show the ways you have been nurturing each ornament.

As you continue your journey, you will discover other gifts that you have.

Draw more ornaments to hang on your special tree.

This is a reminder to always remember the importance of the lessons which Little Garlic learned that can also be lessons to help you grow in your life.

All these gifts symbolized as ornaments will be your companions and you can nurture them each day on your journey.

My Gratitude Journal

Now that you have started your journey, it would be wonderful if you would now continue that journey by starting a "gratitude" practice.

At the end of each day, Little Garlic always thanked Onion for being his friend and for all the lessons he had learned that day.

Each night before you go to bed, review your day, and bring to your mind anything that happened for which you can be grateful.

There are so many things that we can be grateful for at any time. For example, if we can see, if we can hear, if we can walk, if we can smell, if we can feel, if we can appreciate beauty: these are all amazing gifts. Maybe someone smiled at you and made you happy. Maybe someone shared something with you. Maybe you shared something with someone and made someone happy.

There are so many gifts that we can be grateful for each day.

The sun, the moon, the stars, nature, the air you breathe, and so on. They are all gifts that are yours wherever you are.

And being grateful for each thing or each person in your life is a source of strength that will carry you through the day and give you hope, especially during tough times.

If you remember each night all the gifts that you can be grateful for, tomorrow will be a better day.

It might help you to keep a little notebook by your bed. Each night after you review your day, you can write down whatever you can be grateful for that happened during the day and what you hope for tomorrow.

After you have finished thinking and writing about what you are grateful for, see how it feels in your heart to be grateful. Close your eyes and breathe in that feeling of gratitude from your heart and as you exhale let peace, hope, and love embrace you. Rest in that feeling of goodness and tenderness.

Sweet dreams.

We are grateful for you.

Flower of Peace Poem

Peace is a seed planted
in the heart that grows
and blossoms from the
goodness of the heart.

Each day when you
wake up, no matter
how difficult it is,
open your eyes
with the feeling of
love in your heart.
Nurture this love as
you go through the day
with a kind deed for
someone in need,
a smile and kind words
for all those you meet.

Remember, an honest
day's work strengthens
the heart, and love
keeps the heart
tender and soft.

Remember to nurture your
heart with hope, faith,
beauty and love
until the seed of peace
blossoms in your heart, and
becomes the Flower of Peace
that you offer to the world.

Remember,
your words,
your deeds,
your work,
your glance,
even a smile
are the petals
of peace nurtured
each day from the
love in your heart.

Just imagine, if
everyone nurtured
their heart like this,
wouldn't the world
be a peaceful place to live?

Notes

Notes

*Now visit **LittleGarlic.org** for more activities,*
audio meditations, and more!

CPSIA information can be obtained
at www.ICGtesting.com
Printed in the USA
JSHW062005210622
27339JS00001B/1